W9-CXU-401

Matzo
Frogs

Matzo Frogs

Sally Rosenthal

art by David Sheldon

NewSouth Books

Montgomery

One sunny morning, Minnie Feinsilver cooked dinner instead of breakfast.

That night, her favorite cousins were coming to her house for
Shabbat dinner, and she wanted to be ready.

"Oy gevalt, what a mess! Look at the time! What will I feed my cousins?"

What could she do? She had promised to spend the day helping her friend, who was laid up in bed with a broken leg.

Shabbat wouldn't wait for her to cook something new.

Now, next door to Minnie there was a pond, and in that pond lived a colony of frogs. Not just any frogs. Jewish frogs.

There was Sol Frog, Mel Frog, Gilda Frog, Golda Frog, Dinah Frog, Barney Frog ... They had been Minnie's neighbors for a long time.

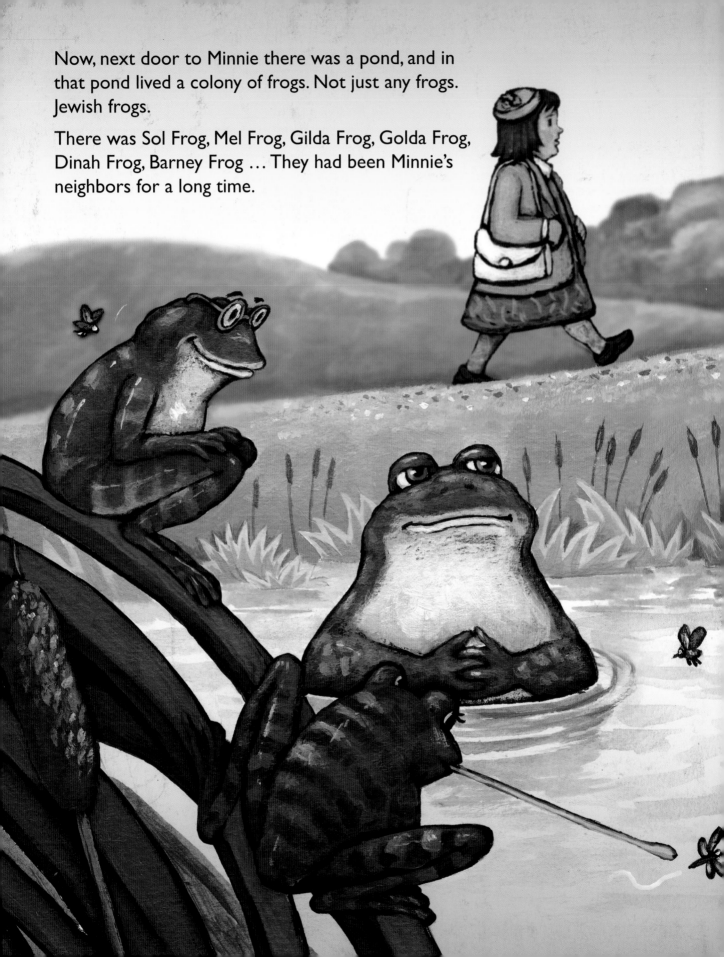

"Poor Minnie."

"We could make the soup so it's ready when she comes home."

"I agree! It would be a mitzvah."

"A mitz-*wha*?"

"A mitzvah. It's an act of kindness."

Everyone knows frogs have long, sticky tongues for catching flies.
But frogs use their tongues for lots of other things too. Like reading.

And grabbing spoons.

And gathering their friends to help.

While the other frogs stirred the broth, one frog worked alone. Sol Frog was an artist. He mixed the matzo meal with a bit of water to make a sticky paste.

"What a fabulous material!" he thought. "Even better than clay." Sol sculpted a dozen matzo balls, but he wondered what else he could create.

He saw the frog in the matzo ball and carved until he set it free.

But how to push the knives through the carrot?

All together they chanted: "One, two, three …

CATAPULT!"

The matzo ball sailed through the air.
First one … PLOP!
Then another … PLOP! PLOP!
Until all of Sol's creations were in
the pot …

PLoP!

PLoP!

PLoP!

They were finished! Almost.

The frogs left the kitchen spotless.

They would sleep well that night.

When Minnie returned from visiting her friend, she found the soup on the stove. It was still warm and smelled heavenly.

"I can't believe it!" she cried. "Shabbat dinner is saved! Who could have done this?"

Minnie whistled as she set the table. Soon after, her cousins arrived.

"Delicious!"

"Minnie, you've outdone yourself!"

"Holy latkes, there's a frog in my soup!"

And then Minnie knew.

That night, before she went to bed, Minnie left a little treat for her friends to enjoy.

"Mitzvah Goreret
Mitzvah."

One mitzvah leads
to another.

For Sophie, my favorite tadpole. — Sally

For W. S. C. — David

NewSouth Books
105 South Court Street
Montgomery, AL 36104

Library of Congress Cataloging-in-Publication Data

Rosenthal, Sally, 1973–
Matzo frogs / Sally Rosenthal ; art by David Sheldon.
pages cm
Summary: As an act of kindness, or mitzvah, six Jewish frogs secretly prepare a delicious pot of matzo ball soup for Minnie Feinsilver's Shabbat dinner. Includes recipe.
ISBN 978-1-58838-302-0 (hardcover)
[1. Frogs—Fiction. 2. Cooking—Fiction. 3. Kindness—Fiction. 4. Judaism—Customs and practices—Fiction.
5. Jews—United States—Fiction.] I. Sheldon, David (David Quentin), illustrator. II. Title.
PZ7.R719448Mat 2014
[E]—dc23

2014000851

A limited-edition paperback has also been produced.
Design by Janice Shay
Printed and bound by Pacom Korea in Gunpo, South Korea
071418.5K1